Ben 10: Annual 2018

A CENTUM BOOK 978-1-911460-75-6

Published in Great Britain by Centum Books Ltd

This edition published 2017

1 3 5 7 9 10 8 6 4 2

Centum Books Ltd, 20 Devon Square, Newton Abbot, Devon, TQ12 2HR, UK

books@centumbooksltd.co.uk

CENTUM BOOKS Limited Reg. No. 07641486

A CIP catalogue record for this book is available from the British Library

Printed in China.

BEN 10

ANNUAL 2018

THIS BOOK BELONGS TO:

_____

_____

FIND 10 SUMO
SLAMMER CARDS
HIDDEN IN
THE BOOK!

WELCOME, ADVENTURE SEEKERS!

Ben and Gwen's epic summer trip with Grandpa Max in the Rustbucket continues with more hikes, museum trips, villains to battle and infinite fun.

Everything changed when Ben found the Omnitrix, now he can transform into any of ten aliens, each with their own unique powers.

You can read about their powers on the fact pages throughout the book. Plus there are loads of fun activities, puzzles, art challenges and stories for you to get stuck into.

But first let's meet everyone...

Rustbucket

Ben

Gwen

Grandpa Max

HERE COME THE ALIENS!

Grey Matter
Page 40

Wildvine
Page 57

Diamondhead
Page 22

Overflow
Page 49

Cannonbolt
Page 13

Four Arms
Page 34

Stinkfly
Page 67

Heatblast
Page 45

Upgrade
Page 64

XLR8
Page 60

Size guide

BEN TENNYSON

Our hero is ten years old. When the Omnitrix blasted down to Earth Ben found it and it's been strapped to his wrist ever since. He is now the wielder of one of the most powerful devices in the universe.

Ben's full name is Benjamin Kirby Tennyson.

Ben is terrified of squids!

He is on a mission to collect all the Sumo Slammer cards.

He loves jokes, pranks and teasing his cousin Gwen.

Not a fan of chores, but will do anything for his Grandpa Max.

GWEN

Gwen is Ben's cousin. She's smart and her quick-thinking often helps Ben when he gets into trouble. She's always got Ben's back and despite their differences they make a great team.

Gwen loves facts and knows a lot about EVERYTHING!

She's awesome at computer games and battles with Ben for high scores.

GRANDPA MAX

Grandpa Max owns the Rustbucket, an awesome motor home, which is Ben and Gwen's home for the summer. He loves planning visits to new places, has a huge sense of adventure and love for the Great Outdoors.

Grandpa Max is a BIG fan of long hikes.

He enjoys visiting obscure places, the weirder the better.

Can you spot Grey Matter in the alien line-up?

See answer on page 74.

PACK IT UP!

Time to get ready for the trip of a lifetime. Ben has made a list of his essential summer-trip items to take on the Rustbucket. Read his list, then make your own below.

★ **Sumo Slammer Cards** (Hopefully I'll find even more)

★ **Computer Games** (Gonna need some entertainment)

★ **Sumo Slammer Comics** (Midnight-reading essentials)

★ **Water Pistol** (To annoy Gwen ☺)

★ **Football** (To play with all the friends I'll meet)

★ **Secret Sweet Stash** (Midnight gaming fuel)

★ **Awesome New Trainers** (For all the hikes Grandpa will make us go on 😖)

What are your must-have items for a big trip? List them here:

BEN 10

CANNONBOLT

FACT FILE

He's big, fierce and you wouldn't want to get in his way. Check out these awesome facts about Cannonbolt.

What's he made of?

Cannonbolt is made of a nearly invulnerable material, which makes him virtually unstoppable.

DID YOU KNOW?

Cannonbolt comes from a planet called Arburia.

Power

He can curl himself up into a ball and roll at fast speeds.

Cannonbolt is way cool!

And big and round!

And he rolls along the ground! Call me a poet.

Watch out!

Sometimes Cannonbolt finds it difficult to stop!

Ball Games

Cannonbolt can turn into an unstoppable ball. Can you name three types of sports balls? Write them in the boxes below.

1 _____

2 _____

3 _____

See answers on page 74.

THE FILTH

1 Out in the desert, something stinky was going down.

2 The Bug Brothers, Maurice and Sydney, were stealing nuclear waste from a truck.

Hmm, do you smell that?

3 "We nearly have enough waste! But we need more... Hmm, do you smell that?" said Maurice, sniffing the air.

4 Meanwhile nearby, Gwen, Grandpa Max and Ben were having a spring clean.

5 They had been cleaning for hours. "Something still stinks!" said Gwen, puzzled.

6 It was Ben. He hadn't cleaned at all. He'd been streaming his favourite TV show instead!

No wifi until you've done your chores.

7 "No wifi until you've done your chores," said Grandpa Max as he left with Gwen to go on a hike.

No problemo!

8 "No problemo!" thought Ben. All he needed to get the job done was some Alien intervention.

9 But trouble was nearby. The Bug Brothers had followed their noses and hatched a plan to steal the stinky Rustbucket.

THWACK!

10

Sydney smacked an unsuspecting XLR8 and the Bug Brothers sped away in their stinky prize.

11

Of course it didn't take XLR8 long to catch up… or be hit again, this time by nuclear sludge. Gross!

12

Ben tried many attacks, but they all seemed to backfire.

13

And when the Omnitrix ran out of juice, Ben hit the road the old-fashioned way, by foot.

DEVASTAION FLATS

98001
INCIDENTS SINCE 1978

CAUTION!
DO
NOT
ENTER

14

Ben followed the Rustbucket's tracks to a nuclear waste facility. It was a really lovely place.

15

OK, it really wasn't. But Ben did make a great discovery – the Rustbucket had been cleaned tyre to roof!

16

All the waste had been pumped into a mysterious machine. What were those Bug Brothers up to?

17

Ben knew it couldn't be anything good. It was probably time for him to start punching things.

18

But before he could throw a punch, Maurice did some punching of his own, punching a button to activate the waste machine!

19 "It's FULLY FUNCTIONAL, SYDNEY! My greatest invention is complete! The Magg-O-NET!" cried Maurice.

20 Then something total yuck happened. A zillion maggots zoomed towards the machine.

21 "Thanks to your disgusting habits, I've reached the final phase of my master plan," Maurice taunted Ben.

Thanks to your disgusting habits...

22 The maggots formed a monster. The Magg-O-NET Monster. It was grosser than Ben's unwashed underpants. And it liked to eat ANYTHING!

CRUNCH!

Do you see Las Vegas over there?

23 "Do you see Las Vegas over there?!?! I want you to eat everything except the money!" Maurice ordered the monster.

24 "So, let me get this straight? You stole our motor home, so you could fuel that trash machine to power a magnet that attracts maggots to make a monster that would eat Las Vegas? Whatever. Time to throw stuff!"

So, let me get this straight?

25

26

27

Ben crunched and smashed the remote control…

…but that was a big mistake. Now the monster was out of control.

The Bug Brothers crawled away scared, leaving Ben to deal with the monster.

28

29

WHAM!

Ben realised there was a magnet powering the monster. He threw the Rustbucket…

…and WHAM, the magnet was blasted away.

30

Ha, ha!

31 There was still one problem, though. The Rustbucket was now covered in maggots. Ben set to work and the Rustbucket was sparkling by the time Gwen and Grandpa Max got back. Grandpa was pleased.

"Ha, ha!" thought Ben. "Now I get it. Maggot, Magg-O-NET!"

Oh man!

32 "You did a great job cleaning, but you have to finish all your chores before you get your wifi back." Grandpa Max told him.

THE END

MEGA MATCH-UP TIME

Ben may have stayed up too late watching Sumo Slammer episodes last night, because he's having trouble working out which shadows belong to which Aliens. Help him out and match them up.

Answers

1 = K   4 = D   7 = I   10 = B
2 = M   5 = L   8 = C   Which shadows don't match any Alien?
3 = A   6 = F   9 = J   G   H   ◯

See answers on page 74.

Tip: There are more shadows here than there are Aliens, so take extra care!

CROSSWORD ALIENS

Solve the clues below to complete this Alien-themed word puzzle.

ACROSS

1 With skin of liquid metal, this Alien can boost and power technology.

5 His DNA is silicon-based and diamond hard.

8 Blink and you'll miss this speedy Alien.

9 Things tend to heat up when this Alien is around.

10 Shoots water from his arms like water pistols.

DOWN

2 The smallest but by no means the weakest Alien in Ben's line-up.

3 Can roll himself into an unstoppable ball.

4 Why have two when you can have four?

6 Keep away from this Alien's flammable goo and slime attack!

7 Baddies often get tangled up in this Alien's attacks.

20

See answers on page 74.

CODED QUESTION

You're going to need all your brainpower to solve this one!

Grey Matter is testing your Ben 10 knowledge, but he's not making it easy for you because he's testing you in code. Use the symbols to work out what he's asking you, then answer his question.

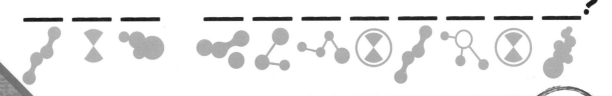

See answer on page 74.

Answer

21

DIAMONDHEAD
FACT FILE

He's shiny, he's big and he's hero ready. Check out these awesome facts about Diamondhead.

What's he made of?

His body is made of green crystals.

DNA

It's silicone-based and diamond hard.

Power

Ben can control Diamondhead's structure and reform it into crystal weapons, from swords to shields.

Diamondhead, more like Pointyhead!

I'd watch out who you call pointy head!

DID YOU KNOW?

Diamondhead comes from a planet called Petropia.

Gem Test

Diamondhead has a gem-inspired name. Can you name three other precious gems? Write them in the boxes below.

1

2

3

See answers on page 74.

CODED COLOURING

Use the code to colour in the Omnitrix and make it look super awesome.

Code

1 2 3
4 5 6

COLOURING TIP

To get a different shade of grey, try pressing harder or lighter with your pencil.

DID YOU KNOW?

Ben found the Omnitrix after it crashed to Earth from space!

FAMILY SEQUENCES

Check out the family snaps below and work out which picture comes next in the sequences.

 A

 B

 C

1

2

3

4

5

See answers on page 74.

VINE TIME

Wildvine is on the attack. Doodle more vines coming from his body and fill the page with wild power.

Tip: Make sure you don't get his vines in a tangle!

Colour in the frame to complete your masterpiece!

POWERS OF OBSERVATION

Villains beware! Ben and Gwen have become really good at spotting when something or someone is up to no good. Test your powers of observation in these spot-the-difference challenges!

CHALLENGE ONE:

EASY

Can you find the **five** differences between these two pictures?

CHALLENGE TWO:

MEDIUM

Now, can you find the **five** differences between these two pictures?

CHALLENGE THREE:

HARD

Finally, can you find the **ten** differences between these two pictures?

See answers on page 74.

Did you find all **twenty** differences? Colour in the gauge to match your score and work out your observation skill level.

20

WINNER

You're SUPER observant!

15

Not much gets past you.

10

Still a bit of work to do.

5

Wake up sleepyhead!

0

27

CREATE YOUR OWN ALIEN

Have you ever imagined yourself as an Alien? Let your imagination go wild on these pages and create an Omnitrix worthy Alien!

CIRCLE THE WORDS THAT APPLY TO YOUR ALIEN:

IS IT...?
BIG
SMALL
SLOW
FAST
SHY
SCARY

DOES IT HAVE...?
HORNS
A TAIL
WINGS
A BEAK
BIG FEET

WHAT PLANET IS IT FROM?

_____

THINK UP A FUN NAME AND WRITE IT HERE:

_____

WHAT'S ITS DNA LIKE?

WRITE ABOUT ITS POWER AND SPECIAL ATTACKS HERE.

DRAW YOUR ALIEN HERE:

Label its special features!

ACTION COLOURING

Check out this awesome battle scene between Four Arms and some mean-looking villains. Make the pages pop by colouring in the pictures.

31

COMIC CREATOR

Imagine you're the star of your very own Ben 10 adventure.
Write, draw and create your own comic-strip story below.

ONE DAY, I WAS IN THE ... *(TICK THE BOX)*

- ☐ CLASSROOM
- ☐ WOODS
- ☐ SUPERMARKET

WHEN AN EVIL VILLAIN CALLED _____ SHOWED UP AND...

DRAW THE VILLAIN HERE!

EVERYONE RAN AWAY BECAUSE... *(WHAT DID THE VILLAIN DO?)*

_____

_____

_____

_____

_____

I SUMMONED _____ FROM THE OMNITRIX. IT WAS TIME TO BATTLE!

DRAW THE ALIEN HERE!

PRESS-OUT SECTION

Have some alien fun with these awesome masks and 3D Omnitrix.

Turn to page 61 for the instructions.

Heatblast

XLRB

2

1

3

THE BATTLE WAS TOUGH, BUT I USED A SPECIAL POWER.

(DESCRIBE WHAT HAPPENED NEXT)

_____

_____

_____

_____

_____

_____

_____

SUDDENLY THE VILLAIN...

(TICK THE BOX)

☐ JUMPED
☐ BURPED
☐ SCREAMED
☐ VANISHED
☐ LAUGHED

DRAW ANOTHER BIT OF THE ACTION HERE.

FROM THAT DAY ON I....

(WRITE THE ENDING HERE!)

_____

_____

_____

_____

_____

_____

_____

THE END!

33

FOUR ARMS

FACT FILE

He's multi-armed, he's strong and he's battle ready. Check out these awesome facts about Four Arms.

DID YOU KNOW?

Four Arms comes from a planet called Khoros.

Four stinky armpits, ewwwwww!

All the better to make gross sounds with!

What's he made of?

His body is made up of pure Alien muscle. POW!

Power

As Four Arms, Ben can lift the heaviest of objects and pack the most powerful of punches.

Watch Out!

His muscles are some of the most powerful in the universe.

The Power of Four

Four Arms thinks that having four arms is really handy! (Ha, ha!) Can you work out how many fingers Four Arms has in total?

Clue: It's 4+4+4+4!

FOUR ARMS HAS _____ FINGERS!

See answers on page 75.

BEN 10

HERO TIME

CAMPSITE CONFUSION

Look at this campsite picture of Ben, Gwen and Grandpa Max. Some of the pieces are missing. Can you work out which pieces complete the picture?

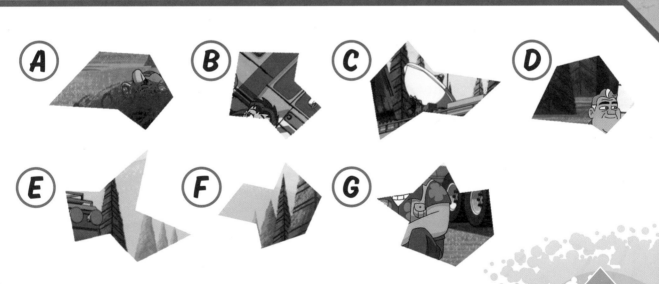

See answers on page 75.

Answers

1 = ◯   3 = ◯

2 = ◯   4 = ◯

Is there someone spying on Ben?

37

FLAMING MAZE

There's only one Alien that can cool down this sizzling situation. Help Overflow find a path through the maze avoiding the hot spots and stop La Grange from making his escape!

START

38

DID YOU KNOW?

La Grange is obsessed with treasure and will do anything to get it, no matter what the cost.

FINISH

See answers on page 75.

GREY MATTER

FACT FILE

He's tiny, he's mighty and he's ready for anything. Check out these awesome facts about Grey Matter.

DID YOU KNOW?

Grey Matter comes from a planet called Galvan Prime.

What's he made of?

Grey Matter is very similar to a frog.

Power

Grey Matter is a tech head, able to see how complex machines work by literally getting inside them.

Watch out!

Despite his small size, he has incredible strength!

 Small, but mighty intelligent!

Hmm, one tenth intelligent you mean.

 I'll take it!

Brain-teaser

Here is a riddle to test your brain cells.

What is as light as a feather, but impossible to hold for more than a few minutes?

40

See answer on page 75.

MUDDLE TROUBLE

Help Four Arms get a grip on this villain by working out which steamed-up line will lead him to Steam Smythe.

See answers on page 75.

STICKY SITUATION

Stinkfly is on the attack. Doodle slime and stinkiness and fill the page with gunge!

Tip: Use shading techniques to make your gunge look 3D!

Colour in the frame to complete your masterpiece!

POWER OF TEN WORDSEARCH

Ben has listed 10 words that are important to him. Can you find them in the grid below? Look across, down and diagonally!

ACTION
ADVENTURE
ALIEN
BATTLE
FAMILY
FUN
HERO
OMNITRIX
POWER
TEN

J	B	A	T	T	L	E	G	A	D	T	Y
W	Z	O	Q	A	U	K	R	F	P	H	C
A	M	S	E	T	C	V	X	U	B	E	F
J	D	H	N	W	I	T	E	N	Q	R	D
P	S	V	H	U	M	A	I	K	L	O	W
A	L	I	E	N	Y	Z	K	O	F	T	B
M	D	A	R	N	U	X	F	J	N	L	E
G	O	M	N	I	T	R	I	X	O	V	P
T	K	R	C	S	H	U	B	A	D	F	O
X	O	Q	F	K	N	E	R	G	Y	P	W
J	F	A	M	I	L	Y	T	E	X	I	E
Y	V	L	B	A	O	L	C	S	U	K	R

Can you write down ten words that are important to you?

1. _____
2. _____
3. _____
4. _____
5. _____
6. _____
7. _____
8. _____
9. _____
10. _____

See answers on page 75.

OUT OF THIS WORLD JOKES

Ben is known to face his enemies with a lot of fun and humour. Read these HA-HA-Larious Alien-inspired jokes and see if you can't help but crack a smile.

What do you call an alien with three eyes?
An aliiiien!

Where do aliens go to school?
Universe-ities!

What's an alien's favourite dance?
Moonwalk

What do you call a spaceship that's upset?
A crying saucer!

What do aliens like to drink?
A nice cup of Gravi-tea!

What do aliens like to read?
Comet Books

How do you get an alien to sleep?
Rocket

What do you say to a two-headed alien?
Hello! Hello!

What do aliens wear to the office?
Space suits!

HEATBLAST

FACT FILE

He's bright, he's blasty and he's flaming hot. Check out these awesome facts about Heatblast.

DID YOU KNOW?

Heatblast comes from a planet called Pyros.

DNA

His DNA is comprised of a magma-like substance that is incredibly hot.

Watch Out!

Heatblast's flame can be put out with water.

Power

Ben has control over all heat-based blasts and is able to throw fire from his hands.

 Heatblast can also burp flames.

 And make popcorn in two seconds!

The Heat is On!

 ▶

Fill in the missing letters on these hot words.

F	L		M	E
	U	R	N	
B		I	L	

See answers on page 75.

45

COPY DRAW

Tip: Press lightly with your pencil at first, so it's easy to rub out.

Cannonbolt

Four Arms

WHICH DRAWING IS YOUR FAVOURITE?

Diamondhead

Heatblast

Tip: Do one square at a time to build up the complete picture.

47

RUSTY DOT-TO-DOT

Grandpa Max's love for the outdoors is probably only matched by his love of the trusty Rustbucket. Complete this dot-to-dot of his beloved truck!

Once you're done, colour it and draw a scene around it!

You could give the Rustbucket a new colourful makeover for fun.

OVERFLOW

He's aqua-powered, he's strong and he's ready to make a splash. Check out these awesome facts about Overflow.

FACT FILE

DID YOU KNOW?

Overflow comes from a planet called Kiusana.

What's he made of?

This alien is a mysterious, liquid-based creature.

Power

Ben has control over most forms of moisture and can shoot water from his arms.

 And no known weaknesses.

Is being annoying a weakness?

 I'd consider it a strength!

Watch Out!

When you can control water, you can control most of the planet!

Ocean Challenge

Can you name three large oceans?

1

2

3

See answers on page 75

49

FREAKY GWEN BEN

1 Grandpa Max was totally psyched about checking out the Swap Meet.

2 Gwen and Ben were too! Grandpa Max gave them each ten whole dollars to spend.

3 "If we put our money together, we could get something super cool!" Gwen cleverly suggested.

4 That was an awesome idea, but they couldn't quite decide on what to get.

Err, no.

5 "What about this?" said Ben. "Err, no. Way scary. And weird!" said Gwen.

6 Meanwhile, the Swap Meet had an unexpected visitor.

7 Hex was tracking down the powerful Titan Gauntlets.

Where are the Titan Gauntlets?

8 "Where are the Titan Gauntlets!" he screamed in frustration.

9 Ben and Gwen were still searching for the perfect purchase when they both met a mysterious market stall owner.

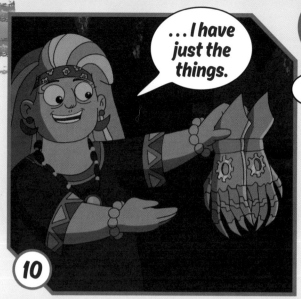

10

"If you're looking for something amazing, cool and powerful," she said. "I have just the things."

11

Gloves?

Really?

"Gloves?" asked Gwen. "Really?" said Ben. They both knew what they really wanted. Gwen had seen some roller skates and Ben wanted a Sumo Slammer Slushy machine. Neither was caving in!

Try walking a moment in each other's shoes.

12

Grandpa Max heard them both arguing. "You've got to try and see eye to eye," he told them. "Try walking a moment in each other's shoes."

13

Suddenly they heard screams. Hex was transforming the market into monsters in his search for the Titan Gauntlets!

14

Hex showed some giant-sized stuffed toys what the Gauntlets looked liked. "Those are the gloves from earlier!" Gwen said with recognition.

15

It's show time!

16

While Gwen and Grandpa Max went off to get the Gauntlets, Ben went to battle Hex. "It's show time!" he cried.

"How far do I have to throw you before you smash?" cried Hex. He had Diamondhead in a curse attack!

17

Diamondhead wasn't working and Ben was out of ideas.

51

18

What are you doing, Ben?

Gwen was not impressed!
"What are you doing, Ben!
You've run out of juice already!"

19

Hex saw Ben and Gwen
arguing and it gave him
an idea for a new curse.

20

10

Ben and Gwen were
zapped by Hex and
something very
strange happened!

21

I don't know how to use the Omnitrix!

Gwen and Ben had swapped
bodies! "I don't know how
to use the Omnitrix!" cried
Gwen in Ben's body.

22

"Not so easy, huh?" said Ben
(as Gwen). "Come on, we've
got to get those gloves."

23

BOOM!

They found the Gauntlets
and Ben (as Gwen) put
on the gloves. They were
super powerful!

24

There you are.

But it only drew Hex's
attention. "There you
are," he cackled.

25

Grey Matter!

Now it was Gwen's turn to
use the Omnitrix. "Grey
Matter!" she cried, but
ended up as Four Arms.

26

Gwen and Ben worked
together to take out Hex...

But Hex didn't stay down for long. Soon he'd stolen the Gauntlets and trapped Ben and Gwen.

"What do we do now?" asked Ben (as Gwen). Hex was destroying the market.

"I've got a plan," said Gwen, "And we're gonna need Upgrade. But can you talk me through it?"

Imagine yourself as water!

"Imagine yourself as water!" said Ben. Gwen slithered out of the cursed ropes and made her way to Hex.

Gwen turned towards Hex, who was about to blast away an entire mountain!

Gwen sneaked up on Hex...

...and destroyed the Titan Gauntlets!

Hex found himself a bit tied up and very much in trouble. Ben and Gwen found that teamwork really did pay off!

THE END

53

COUNTER ATTACK!

WHOA! There are so many Alien counters on these pages. Count them up and write their totals on the right. Once you're done, answer the questions around the page!

BEN 10

Which Alien appears the most?

Design your own counter in this circle!

Which Alien appears the least?

Which Alien appears ten times?

Ben 10
Omnitrix
Upgrade
Heatblast
Overflow
Diamondhead
Wildvine
Cannonbolt
XLR8
Four Arms
Grey Matter
Stinkfly

See answers on page 75.

55

WILDVINE

He's wild, he's green and he's mean. Check out these awesome facts about Wildvine.

FACT FILE

DID YOU KNOW?

Wildvine comes from a planet called Flors Verdance.

What's he made of?

Awesome adaptable plant material.

Watch Out!

Ben has to be careful not to get his vines tangled up.

That collar is the height of Flors Verdance fashion!

No it's not! You need some hedge clippers!

Power

Ben can merge with any plant on the planet and can grow and retract arms and vines at will.

Plant Life

Can you name the type of forest that is home to most of the world's species of plants (and animals!)? Fill in the missing letters.

| | A | I | N | | O | R | E | | T |

See answer on page 76.

57

VILLAINS IN OLDEVILLE

Ben and Gwen thought their stop in Oldeville was going to be boring, but it is absolute chaos! Everywhere you look there are villains. Search the scene and find them all.

Vilgax

Steam Smythe

Zombozo

Dr Animo

Bounty Hunter

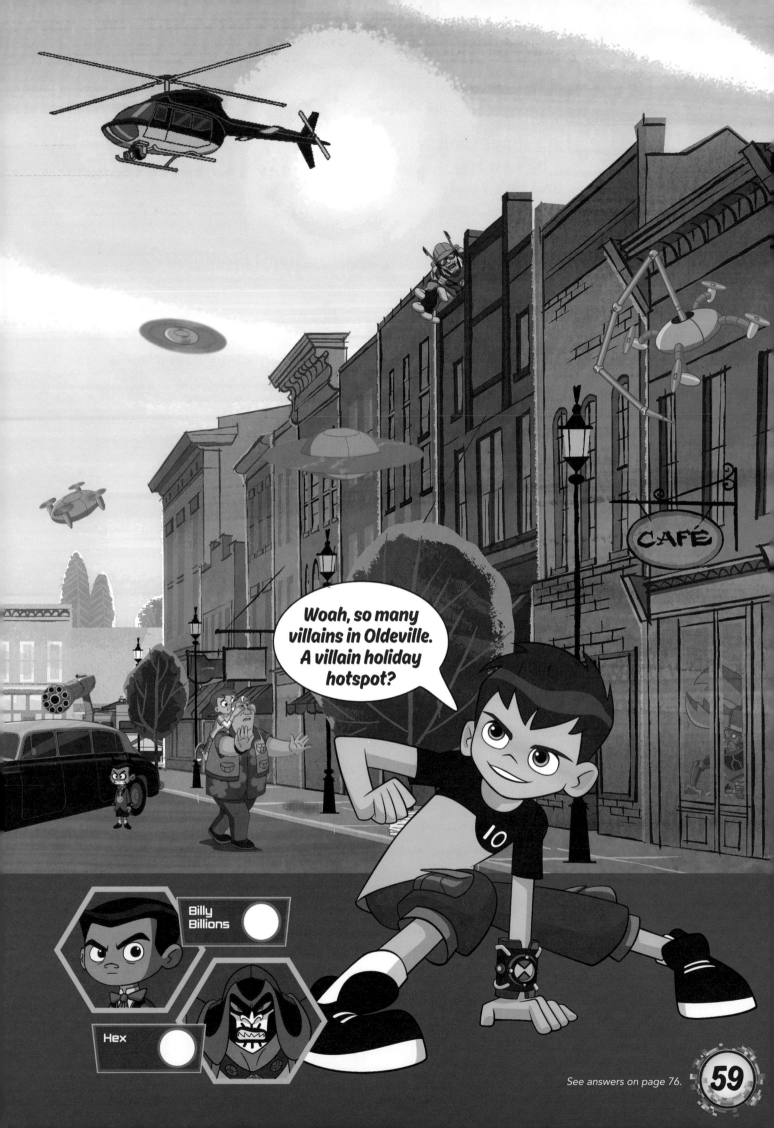

XLR8

He's super-sonic, he's strong and he's ready to race. Check out these awesome facts about XLR8.

FACT FILE

DID YOU KNOW?

XLR8 comes from a planet called Kinet.

What's he made of?

He's made of matter which can tolerate 500 mph speeds.

Watch Out!

XLR8 better be fast, as strength is not a strong suit for this alien form.

Power

Ben is the super speedster alien and can travel at crazy high speeds!

Why do you have bowling feet?

Why do you always act like a baby?

I don't act like a baby. I don't I don't I don't!

Animal Speed

Fill in the missing letters to reveal the name of the speediest Earth animal on land.

Did you know that this animal can run at over 60 mph?

C	H	E		E		T		H

See answers on page 76.

PRESS-OUT INSTRUCTIONS

Have you found the press-out card section in this book containing masks and your very own Omnitrix? The pieces are easy to assemble, just follow these instructions.

AWESOME OMNITRIX

Step One:
To make the Omnitrix's face, first take parts 1 and 2 and fold down all the tabs. Next, slot the tab on part 1 with the red dot on, into the slit on part 2 between the two tabs with the red dots on. Curve part 1 around part 2, slotting the tabs on part 1 into the slits on part 2.

Step Two: To attach the face to the strap, slot the long tabs from part 1 into middle slits on part 3. The tab with the blue dot should go through the blue slit.

Step Four:
Place the strap on your wrist and roll the edges of the strap under and slot the tab into the slit to fit your wrist.

Step Three:
Fold the tabs inwards, then slot the ends back up into the inner slits on part 3.

AMAZING MASKS

Step One: To make a mask, first press out the mask piece and press-out the holes.

Step Two: Cut two pieces of string or ribbon of equal length. Approx 30 cm each.

Step Three: Take the first piece of string and thread it through the holes on one side and tie in place. Repeat on the other side.

Step Four: Now position the mask on your face and ask a grown-up to help you fix it in place by tying the two pieces of string or ribbon together behind the back of your head. Strike your best Alien pose!

You will need:
Press-out masks
String or ribbon
Scissors

TRAVELLING TRIO

Ben, Gwen and Grandpa Max are on the road again on their way to a cool campsite. (Well, Ben and Gwen hope it is!) Help Grandpa Max navigate the best route for the Rustbucket, avoiding the villains along the way.

START

CONTINUE

FINISH

See answers on page 76.

63

UPGRADE

He's mysterious, he's adaptable and he's ready to take charge. Check out these awesome facts about Upgrade.

FACT FILE

DID YOU KNOW?

Upgrade comes from a moon called Galvan.

Upgrade's colours are violet and indigo.

Don't you mean purple and purple?!

What's he made of?

Upgrade is a "mechamorph" – a living machine with liquid metallic skin.

Power

His nanotechnological body can pour itself over any piece of technology, merge with it and upgrade it to something more powerful.

Upgrade the Rustbucket

Doodle and colour Upgrade's skin patterns over this picture of the Rustbucket!

STINKFLY

He's fast, he can fly and he's ready to make a stink. Check out these awesome facts about Stinkfly.

FACT FILE

DID YOU KNOW?

Stinkfly comes from a planet called Lepidopterra.

Power

The liquid goos and gases he shoots from his eyes and mouth possess a wide range of powers.

I'm not sure Stinkfly smells any worse than your old underwear.

Let's do a test... on you!

What's he made of?

Stinkfly is similar to a glowing insect.

Watch Out!

Some of the goo is highly flammable!

Buzz Off!

Fill in the missing letters on these buzzy insects' names.

W		S	P

U	M	B	L		B		E

D		A	G	O	N		L	Y

See answers on page 76.

RUSTBUCKET RIP

1

Ben and Gwen were not too pumped by the thought of visiting Oldeville.

2

CARDS N GAMEZ

Although Ben perked up when he spotted a shop selling a rare Sumo Slammer Card.

3

Can we go? Can we go? Can we go?

"Can we go? Can we go? Can we go?" Ben cried. "Maybe later," replied Grandpa Max, "I've got a whole list of things planned."

4

No way!

"No way! I need that card – there's only one!" said Ben.

5

"Tell you what, Ben, you can either spend the day exploring Oldeville, not using your powers, or spend the day doing chores, not using your powers."

6

"Chores, please!" said Ben. "Me too!" said Gwen.

7

Grandpa Max went off on his first tour of the day. Instantly Ben transformed into XLR8.

8

That's cheating, Ben!

"That's cheating, Ben!" said Gwen. "I'll be back soon – gotta collect me a card!" said Ben.

9

Someone else was also speeding after the card...the youngest super-villain in the world. Billy Billions!

10 Ben beat Billy to the shop and got the card! What a result!

11 But Billy wasn't happy about it. "I want that card," cried Billy. "And I always get what I want!"

12 Ben wouldn't give it up, so Billy decided to steal the Rustbucket.

13 Bad timing! Grandpa Max was returning from a tour.

14 Gwen and Ben needed to distract Grandpa Max fast. So they hopped on another tour with him.

15 "I'm going to go and do something," said Ben, sneaking off the bus and changing into Wildvine.

16 Ben had spotted Billy driving away. "It's wild time!" he cried, chasing after Billy.

17 Using his vine attack, Ben closed in on the Rustbucket.

18 But Billy was prepared. "Time to test out my special tech attacks!" said Billy, activating a panel.

"Dodge this if you can! It's the best tech that money can buy!"

Wildvine struggled with Billy's machine, but crushed it with his plant power.

Luckily Grandpa Max didn't notice as Ben sped by!

With the Omnitrix out of juice, Ben ducked inside the Rustbucket.

He zapped Billy's tech with water – if only he could turn into Overflow!

Overflow!

When the Omnitrix recharged, Ben called out "Overflow!" but he got Heatblast instead.

Billy was ready to strike again and sent more tech Ben's way.

"Why do I never get the Alien I really need?" said Ben, as Billy attacked again.

Ben spotted a fire hydrant and blasted it! Water burst out and destroyed the tech.

28 Billy was so annoyed that he started to blast up the town. "I may not like this town," said Ben, "but you really need to stop that now!"

29 Ben blasted Billy's car and the legs began to break.

30 Finally, Heatblast zapped Billy's car in two.

31 Billy threw a tantrum. "I JUST WANT THAT CARD," he bawled.

32 Things only got worse for Billy when his super-villain parents turned up.

33 "So all of this was about a card?" said Grandpa Max. "I have the perfect solution." He ripped the card in two.

"I will get my revenge!" cried Billy as his parents dragged him away.

35 "Looks like we'll be staying in Oldeville until the Rustbucket is fixed," said Gwen. "Please don't make me go to the Dust Museum!" said Ben.

THE END **71**

ULTIMATE QUIZ

Study the pictures and answer the questions in this ultimate Ben 10 quiz. Not sure of an answer? Well, have another look through the book to refresh your memory.

1 Which Alien shoots stinky slime?

A.

B.

C.

D.

2 Which picture doesn't show Overflow?

A.

B.

C.

D.

3 Which Alien can curl up into a ball?

A.

B.

C.

D.

4 Which Alien can travel at over 500 mph?

A.

B.

C.

D.

5 Which picture doesn't show Upgrade?

A.

B.

C.

D.

6 Which Alien is made of magma?

A.

B.

C.

D.

7 Which Alien is the smallest?

A.

B.

C.

D.

8 Which Alien can shoot water from his arms?

A.

B.

C.

D.

9 Which Alien has silcon-based DNA?

A.

B.

C.

D.

10 Which one is the villain?

A.

B.

C.

D.

ANSWERS

P 5

Sumo Slammer cards are on pages: 8, 10, 18, 23, 32, 38, 44, 56, 63, 69.

P 8

Grey Matter is here.

P 13

Did you get any of these suggestions?
FOOTBALL, TENNIS BALL, PING-PONG BALL, GOLF BALL, BASKETBALL, NETBALL, SNOOKER BALL, BOWLING BALL, BASEBALL, to name a few ...

P 18

1. = K;	2. = M;	3. = A;	4. = D;
5. = L;	6. = E;	7. = I;	8. = C;
9. = F;	10. = B		

The shadows that don't match any Aliens are: G, H, J.

P 20

Across:
1. UPGRADE
5. DIAMONDHEAD
8. XLR8
9. HEATBLAST
10. OVERFLOW

Down:
2. GREYMATTER
3. CANNONBALL
4. FOURARM
6. STINKFLY
7. WILDVINE

P 21

How many Aliens are in the Omnitrix?
Answer: 10.

P 22

Did you get any of these suggestions?
RUBY, SAPPHIRE, EMERALD.

P 24

1. C; **2.** A; **3.** C; **4.** B; **5.** B.

P 26

1. Easy

2. Medium

3. Hard

74

P 34

Four Arms has sixteen fingers!

P 37

1. C; **2.** E; **3.** G; **4.** A.
Dr Amino is spying on Ben.

P 38–39

P 40

"Your breath!"

P 41

Line **3** leads to Steam Smythe.

P 43

J	B	A	T	T	L	E	G	A	D	T	Y
W	Z	O	Q	A	U	K	R	F	P	H	C
A	M	S	E	T	C	V	X	U	B	E	F
J	D	H	N	W	I	T	E	N	Q	R	D
P	S	V	H	U	M	A	I	K	L	O	W
A	L	I	E	N	Y	Z	K	O	F	T	B
M	D	A	R	N	U	X	F	J	N	L	E
G	O	M	N	I	T	R	I	X	O	V	P
T	K	R	C	S	H	U	B	A	D	F	O
X	O	Q	F	K	N	E	R	G	Y	P	W
J	F	A	M	I	L	Y	T	E	X	I	E
Y	V	L	B	A	O	L	C	S	U	K	R

P 45

FLAME
BURN
BOIL

P 49

The Pacific Ocean, Atlantic Ocean, Southern Ocean, Indian Ocean, Arctic Ocean.

P 55

 4 10

 6 9

 7 7

 5 3

2 13

 6 4

Grey Matter appears the most.
Overflow appears the least.
Wildvine appears ten times.

P 56

Overflow **4.** is Hex in disguise.

P 57

RAINFOREST

P 58-59

P 60

CHEETAH

P 61-62

P 67

WASP
BUMBLEBEE
DRAGONFLY

P 72

1. B;   **2.** A;   **3.** D;   **4.** C;   **5.** D;
6. B;   **7.** C;   **8.** A;   **9.** D;   **10.** B.

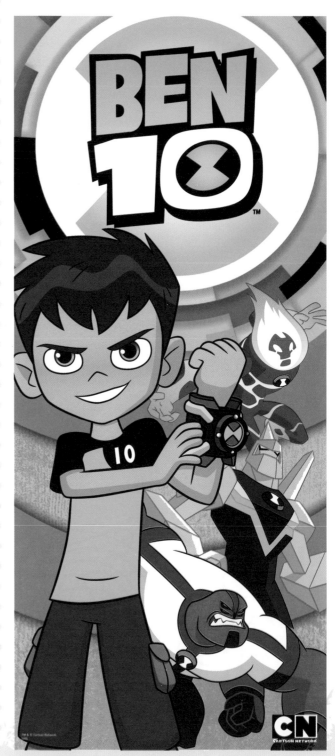

BEN 10 GALLERY

Use this page to stick in pictures and selfies of you wearing your Ben 10 masks and Omnitrix!